That's When I Talk to God

Dan & Ali Morrow
Illustrated by Cory Godbey

David C Cook®
transforming lives together

THAT'S WHEN I TALK TO GOD
Published by David C Cook
4050 Lee Vance View
Colorado Springs, CO 80918 U.S.A.

David C Cook Distribution Canada
55 Woodslee Avenue, Paris, Ontario, Canada N3L 3E5

David C Cook U.K., Kingsway Communications
Eastbourne, East Sussex BN23 6NT, England

David C Cook and the graphic circle C logo
are registered trademarks of Cook Communications Ministries.

This story is a work of fiction. All characters and events are the product of the author's
imagination. Any resemblance to any person, living or dead, is coincidental.

Unless otherwise noted, all Scripture quotations are taken from the *New American Standard Bible*, ©
Copyright 1960, 1995 by The Lockman Foundation. Used by permission. Scripture quotations marked
NIV are taken from the Holy Bible, New International Version®, NIV®. Copyright © 1973, 1978, 1984 by
Biblica, Inc™. Used by permission of Zondervan. All rights reserved worldwide. www.zondervan.com.

LCCN 2010942613
ISBN 978-1-4347-0018-6
eISBN 978-0-7814-0620-8

© 2011 Daniel Morrow and Alison Strobel Morrow
The authors are represented by MacGregor Literary.

The Team: Don Pape, Susan Tjaden, Amy Kiechlin, Caitlyn York, Karen Athen
Cover and Interior Illustrations: Cory Godbey. Art is © David C Cook.

Manufactured in Shen Zhen, Guang Dong, P.R. China, in January 2011 by Printplus Limited.
First Edition 2011

1 2 3 4 5 6 7 8 9 10

121710

The next morning was bright and sunny. I was so excited because my first soccer game was that afternoon! "What a beautiful day," Mom said as she opened the curtains.

"Yeah—and look at the garden. The flowers are so pretty!"

"God really is a great artist, isn't He? I love that about Him," Mom said.

"I love that about God too."

"Why don't you tell Him?" asked Mom.

That's when I can talk to God, I realized, *when I want to tell Him how much I love Him.* I looked out the window at the colorful flowers, the bright blue sky, and the puffy white clouds and said, "I love You, God! You made such a great world for us. You're really good at making things."

After breakfast I went out to play with my best friend, Gwen. Her dad helped us set up a tent so we could pretend we were camping. All morning we imagined her backyard was the forest. We went fishing in her sandbox and roasted marshmallows over a pretend campfire.

"You two are such good friends," Gwen's mom said when we went in for lunch. "Aren't you glad you have each other to play with?"

"Yeah!" I said. "I love Gwen."

That's when I can talk to God, I realized, *when I think of something to be thankful for!* So I prayed, "God, thank You for my friend Gwen."

After lunch I went to my first soccer game. *KICK!* I scored the first goal! I was so excited! "I did it! I'm the best soccer player in the world!" I yelled.

My coach came over to me. "That's not a very good attitude," he said. "You scored because the rest of your team helped you out. You should apologize to them."

"I'm sorry, everybody," I said.

That's when I can talk to God, I realized, *when I need to tell Him I'm sorry*. So I whispered, "God, I'm sorry I was bragging. Please forgive me and help me to have a better attitude."

"So what did you think of your first game?" Mom asked as we drove home from soccer.

"It was so much fun," I said. "But I had a bad attitude and had to tell everyone I was sorry. I told God I was sorry too."

"You did?" she asked. "So you prayed to Him—that's great!"

Suddenly a police car went zooming by, its siren screaming.

When we turned the corner, we saw the police car—and a fire truck, too. They were parked next to a car that had crashed into a tree.

"I hope everyone is okay," I said.

"Maybe we should pray for them," suggested Mom.

That's when I can talk to God, I realized, *when I want to ask Him to help others.* "God, please take care of the people in that car and make everything okay for them," I prayed.

After we got home, my big brother Ollie took me to the park. There's a really big twirly slide that he likes to ride. He kept going up and down, up and down. I wanted to go down too, but I was too scared.

"Come on up with me," he said.

"No way."

Ollie shook his head. "You just need some courage."

That's when I can talk to God, I realized, *when I need Him to help me.* I closed my eyes and said, "God, I don't want to be scared. Please help me to be brave."

Ollie took my hand and led me to the slide. "Come on," he said.

"We'll slide together."

We climbed up, up, up the ladder. When we reached the top, I got scared again. We were so high!

Then Ollie took me on his lap, and we went down, down, down all the way to the bottom. I was so happy.

"I did it!" I shouted. "Thank You, God, for making me brave!"

Soon my friend Joey showed up. "Can you come to my birthday party on Sunday?" Joey asked.

"I can't," I said. "I go to church on Sunday."

"You go to church? Church is dumb!" Joey laughed as he walked away.

I asked Ollie, "Why did he say that?"

"Some people don't believe in God," Ollie told me, "and they think it's silly that we go to church."

That's when I can talk to God, I realized, when I meet people who don't believe in Him. "God, I don't think Joey knows You," I prayed. "Please tell him who You are."

I smelled cookies when we walked back into the house. I asked Mom for one, but she said, "No, we'll be eating dinner soon. You can have one for dessert."

I really wanted one of those yummy cookies. I just couldn't wait! When she wasn't looking, I grabbed one from the counter and took it to my room.

I ate the cookie quickly, before Mom could find out. It was *soooo* good. But then I felt bad. I knew I shouldn't have taken a cookie after Mom said no, but now it was too late.

I needed to tell her what I had done, so I went back to the kitchen and confessed. "I'm sorry, Mom. I took a cookie."

Mom gave me a hug. "Thanks for telling me," she said. "I forgive you."

That's when I can talk to God, I realize, when I've done something I shouldn't have and feel bad. "I'm sorry," I whispered to God. "Please forgive me for not listening to my mom.

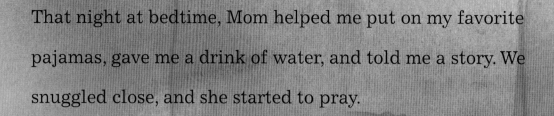

That night at bedtime, Mom helped me put on my favorite pajamas, gave me a drink of water, and told me a story. We snuggled close, and she started to pray.

"Wait, Mom," I said. "Can I pray tonight?"

"Of course," she said.

I closed my eyes and prayed, "God, this was a good day. I love talking to You. Please help me have happy dreams, and give us a good day tomorrow. Amen."

But I had one more question to ask before I fell asleep.

"Mom, does God ever talk to us?"

She smiled and nodded. "Yes, He does. He might not use His voice the way you and I would, but He speaks to people in lots of different ways. Sometimes He uses other people, like when your coach asked you to apologize at soccer. Or through our conscience—the feelings we get that make us want to do the right thing—like when you ate the cookie, then knew it was wrong."

"He talked to me two times today?" I felt so special.

"Are there any other ways He talks to us?"

Mom grinned. "There sure are!"

She reached over and picked up a big book. "God speaks most clearly through His Word, the Bible. That's where He tells us how to treat others, how much He loves us, and what His plans are for us."

"I want to see what God has to say to me," I said. "Can we read the Bible now?"

"Of course we can! We'll start on page one." Mom cleared her voice and began to read. "'In the beginning, God made the heavens and the earth....'"

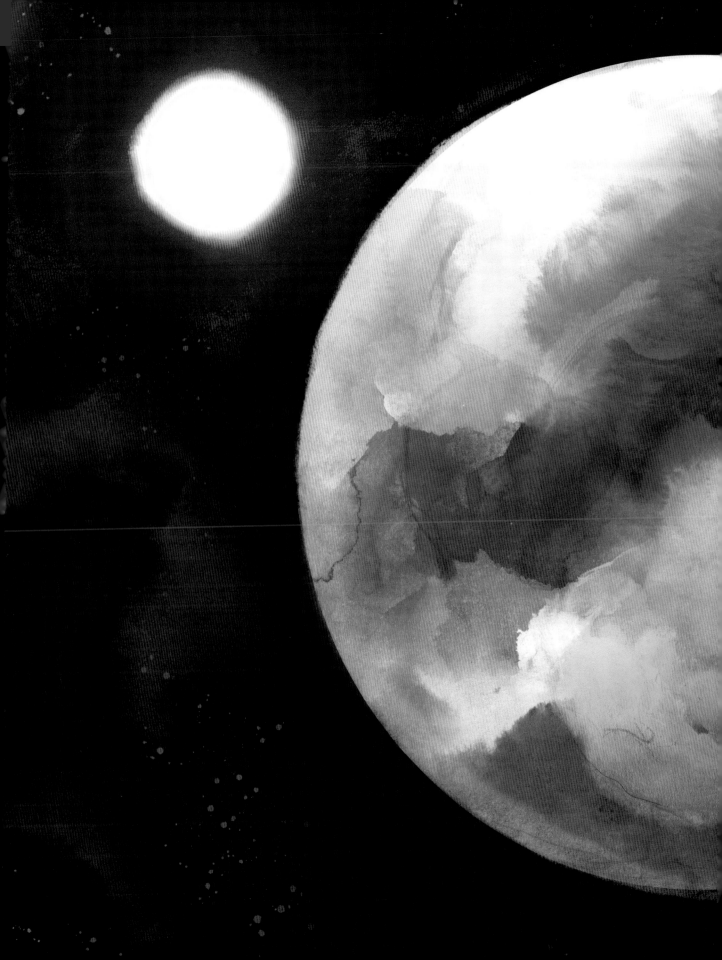

Be joyful always; pray continually; give thanks in all circumstances, for this is God's will for you in Christ Jesus.

1 Thessalonians 5:16–18 (NIV)

Do not be anxious about anything, but in everything, by prayer and petition, with thanksgiving, present your requests to God. And the peace of God, which transcends all understanding, will guard your hearts and your minds in Christ Jesus.

Philippians 4:6–7 (NIV)

Pray then like this:

Our Father who is in heaven,

Hallowed be Your name.

Your kingdom come

Your will be done,

On earth as it is in heaven.

Give us this day our daily bread.

And forgive us our debts, as we also
have forgiven our debtors.

And do not lead us into temptation, but deliver
us from evil. For Yours is the kingdom and
the power and the glory forever. Amen.

Matthew 6:9–13

A Letter from a Grandpa

Dear parent (or grandparent),

One of the greatest joys of being a grandfather to Dan and Ali's daughters, Abigail and Penelope, is getting into conversations with them. Abby the activist tells me about her dance class or going on a hike through the Colorado woods with her dad. Penny the philosopher puzzles over why the sky is blue and confides in me how much she loves her sister. I never tire of listening to their unique observations, questions, and stories.

And if I love to listen to Abby and Penny, how much more must God enjoy the times when they talk with Him in prayer! I can only imagine how He treasures those moments when they converse with Him throughout their days, sharing their lives in innocent and unedited ways.

I hope that this wonderful book, *That's When I Talk to God,* will inspire and motivate your children (or grandchildren) to develop their own vibrant prayer lives. I know that they'll be eager to talk with God after they hear the story of a little girl who learns how she can speak to God anytime she wants—and discovers that He communicates back to her through other people, her conscience, and the Bible.

So let me offer a simple prayer for your young one: May he or she experience the joy and wonder of speaking with the Creator of the universe. And through this, may God knit your child's heart together so that he or she might enjoy a lifetime—and an eternity—of knowing Him personally.

—**Lee Strobel**